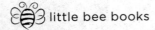 little bee books

New York, NY
Text copyright © 2022 by Cort Lane
Illustrations copyright © 2022 by Little Bee Books
All rights reserved, including the right of reproduction
in whole or in part in any form.
Library of Congress Cataloging-in-Publication Data
is available upon request.
For information about special discounts on bulk purchases,
please contact Little Bee Books at sales@littlebeebooks.com.
Manufactured in China   RRD 0622
ISBN 978-1-4998-1298-5 (paperback)
First Edition 10 9 8 7 6 5 4 3 2 1
ISBN 978-1-4998-1299-2 (hardcover)
First Edition 10 9 8 7 6 5 4 3 2 1
ISBN 978-1-4998-1300-5 (ebook)

littlebeebooks.com

MONSTER AND ME

THE UNICORN'S SPELL

BY CORT LANE

ILLUSTRATED BY
ANKITHA KINI

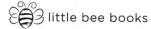
little bee books

Contents

Chapter 1:
Monsters Attack!

Freddy von Frankenstein stood bold and brave, even though he was surrounded by terrifying monsters. It was the most thrilling and chilling moment of his young life. Fortunately, his big brother and best friend, F.M., was by his side. And his brother was "Frankenstein's Monster," perhaps the most powerful monster of all.

The brothers stood back-to-back, ready to take them all on.

A creepy mummy wrapped in rotting bandages stumbled toward them.

A swamp creature dripping with grimy goop rose out of some ooze.

A chupacabra flashed its razor-sharp teeth at them.

The magical yaksha named Uday that Freddy and F.M. had defeated weeks ago was there too.

Worse yet, the giant yeti from their first fantastical encounter was also there, roaring with hunger!

"And watch out for that little guy too," Freddy warned, pointing out a tiny man with a red hat and big beard.

"Ha!" laughed Freddy's father, Victor von Frankenstein. "Gnomes aren't scary!"

Freddy's sister, Riya, asked, "What's a gnome?"

"Hey, I'm trying to give a presentation here!" Freddy complained in frustration. "*All* supernatural creatures can be threats!" Freddy pointed at pictures of all the monsters projected on the wall of Victor's laboratory. Victor turned on the lights and turned off the projector.

"Gnomes are friendly little forest creatures, Riya. It seems that Freddy ran out of ideas for scary monsters."

"Well, you get the idea!" Freddy shot back. "Now can I explain my plan?"

Victor sighed and said, "You only have a few minutes. I'm in the middle of a delicate experiment with my mega-magnetomotor. The magnetic ray charge is almost too big!" Freddy's dad was maybe the smartest scientist in the world. His lab was full of amazing inventions he was always testing out.

Freddy rushed through his speech as fast as he could, "Well, we've already had two monsters show up on the mountain: a yeti and a yaksha."

"And Riya too! She turns into a tiger, after all," added F.M.

"Riya too," Freddy agreed. "That's THREE fantasticals in just a few weeks, which means more are sure to show up! Riya mentioned that something drew her here to our mountain. If she's right, then there could be other fantasticals on their way right now! So, I want to create a team as an extra-credit project. F.M. and I will go on patrol to find any that wind up here. We're the Supernatural Action Search Squad!"

Freddy eagerly looked at everyone to see what they thought of his idea.

Chapter 2:
The Supernatural Action Search Squad

F.M. got a big grin and jumped up and down. "I love meeting new monsters!"

But Riya frowned because it seemed like Freddy thought these "fantasticals" were all trouble. Victor thought for a bit and said, "I know you're a little scared of fantasticals . . ."

Freddy protested, "I'm not scared." F.M. and Riya smiled at each other because they knew Freddy was more afraid than he would admit. Victor continued, "But this doesn't really sound like schoolwork to me. And since I'm in charge of your homeschooling, I don't think this is how you should spend your time. You're always coming up with extra-credit projects like this instead of doing your ACTUAL homework."

Freddy pouted and started to protest, but Victor added, "I'm so busy in my lab these days, I can't always be interrupted with these crazy extra-credit plans of yours. I'm beginning to think we should put you in school down in the village."

Oh no! Not regular school down in the town at the bottom of the mountain, thought Freddy. *That wouldn't be fun at all!* Freddy quickly changed the subject back to his plan to avoid THAT idea. "I've got the squad project all figured out though!"

Freddy unveiled the secret handshake to everyone, which was way too complicated. F.M. messed up and laughed at himself. Even Freddy lost track of some of the steps and got frustrated, making Riya giggle. Victor was unimpressed.

"And I've already made special tech for our search," Freddy continued. "Check out our team badges!" Freddy tried to show one off, but the badge zoomed out of his hand, across the room, and clanked onto F.M.'s forehead. F.M. tried to look up at the badge, confused.

Victor laughed. "Oops, guess my magnetic ray charge must be too strong, because that badge attached to the metal plate in his head!" Riya stifled another laugh. This presentation was not going quite how Freddy had hoped.

"So far I'm not seeing anything that involves homework," warned Victor.

"Well, then you're gonna love this!" Freddy boasted. "Check out our upgraded, high-tech wrist communicators!"

"So, how is any of this really going to help track fantasticals?" Riya asked.

Freddy rolled his eyes. "I can't believe you don't know the kinds of things that super secret clubs need."

Riya looked confused. "But you just told us about it; how can it be a secret?"

Freddy paused and thought. "Uh, well, because, huh . . . Well, here's a wrist communicator of your own!" he said, changing the subject.

"Yeah, try it on!" F.M. said. "This one is too small for my wrists."

Riya was dazzled. "Wow, thanks, Freddy!"

Freddy, continuing with his presentation, proudly announced, "Finally, best of all, I've built a long-distance motion sensor. If someone shows up on the mountain, we can check out if they are a fantastical!"

Victor nodded his head and admitted, "Well, an invention like that actually sounds worthy of *some* extra credit. All right, you win. Go test it out. If it works, we can make this an extra-credit assignment!"

"YAAAYYY!" shouted Freddy.

"But only if your brother goes with you!" warned Victor. "And I'm serious about you doing all your regular homework too. If you can't keep up with all of it, we might need to put you in a real school."

I'd better get out of here before Dad talks any more about school, thought Freddy. So he quickly pushed F.M. out of the lab. "Gotta go test out my sensor tech!" he said while running out of the house.

Victor turned to Riya and asked, "Could you please keep an eye on them too? You're the oldest, and with the sun setting, your tiger powers and cool head will come in handy." Riya felt proud that Victor trusted her. She nodded and ran out to follow her new brothers.

Chapter 3:
Sneaky Surprises

ZOOM! Freddy and F.M. patrolled the mountain on their super-cycle. The mountain they lived on was so high in the Himalayas that there was snow on it much of the year. And it was especially icy and windy today. Freddy loved riding around on the jet-powered vehicle he invented. F.M., who was afraid of high speeds, moaned and held on tight.

Freddy yelled, "Okay, turn the motion sensor on to see if it can find anyone on the mountain!" F.M. pulled the device out of Freddy's tech backpack and flipped the switch.

DING! The sensor immediately found something! The motion was found climbing up the steep, rocky backside of the mountain. Freddy was super excited his device worked!

"What if it's some human mountain climbers?" worried F.M. He had always been afraid of humans, ever since they didn't accept him when Victor created him.

"People never climb up that side of the mountain. They come up the front side, where it's easier. So that means it must be someone up to no good!"

What human would choose to sneak up such a difficult way? Freddy thought. *It must be a monster.* "Looks like the S.A.S.S. has its first case!" shouted Freddy. He sped down to investigate.

***

Meanwhile, Riya struggled to keep up with them. Freddy was driving so fast that they disappeared from her view! But the sun started to set, and she was finally able to turn into her tiger form. Her werecat curse gave her amazing tiger powers, and one of those powers allowed her to run very fast.

"Aha! I'll be able to catch up to them now and make sure they don't get into trouble," said Riya.

To track them, she listened with her amazing cat ears for the sound of the super-cycle. But she also could hear another unfamiliar sound directly down the mountain.

Hmmmm. That sounds like an animal in pain, thought Riya. *What should I do? Check on Freddy and F.M. or help the creature?*

Riya kept running until she could see the super-cycle come into view. She could also see what they were driving toward. *That just looks like a human climbing up the slope. I'll bet F.M. can easily protect Freddy from the climber if he needs to*, thought Riya. *If I run like the wind, I can help the animal and then quickly join the boys in no time.*

As she raced down the mountain, Riya approached the edge of town, and the sound grew louder. There she could see what looked like a horse. Its hoof was trapped in a fence.

Oh no! That fence belongs to the school! The children are playing in the schoolyard after classes, thought Riya. *If they see me, they'll be scared of a tiger. I'm going to have to be super quick!*

As the horse struggled to get free, Riya noticed a glint in the moonlight. She could see a beautiful horn on its head. *A unicorn?! It IS another fantastical. Freddy was right—well, about me being right that fantasticals are drawn to this mountain.* Riya ran even faster to get to the scared unicorn.

Halfway up the mountain, Freddy and F.M. drove up to the mountain climber. *VROOM!* The super-cycle roared to a stop, startling the man.

"Aaaaaah!" the stranger shouted as he started to slide back down the ice. Both brothers were disappointed, but for different reasons.

Aw, bummer. The S.A.S.S. was supposed to find a monster, thought Freddy.

"Oh no!" said F.M. "It's just a man." F.M. hoped the stranger wasn't shouting because he feared him.

"Well, we'd better help him before he falls down the mountain," said Freddy.

Freddy grabbed an invention in his backpack with a robotic arm and grappling hook. The hook caught the man just as he was about to slide off the cliff. "I'll pull him up!" said F.M., using his monster strength to pull the man to safety.

The stranger looked shocked to come face-to-face with the hulking F.M. But to their surprise, he smiled and held out his hand.

"I've waited nine years to meet you!" the stranger said. He took off his hood and goggles, and both F.M. and Freddy looked at each other in shock. This stranger looked exactly like their dad!

Chapter 4:
Uncle Ernst

The man turned to a wide-eyed Freddy and said, "Hello, Freddy! I'm your uncle, Ernst."

Freddy thought, *Wow! He looks just like Dad, except his mustache is skinny and curly.*

Freddy yelped with joy to meet new family. Even F.M. was happy to meet a not-scary human! "You boys sure did save me! What a great way to finally meet my brave, adventurous nephews!" said Ernst. Their uncle gave them a wide grin.

"So, why are you here? How come we've never met you before? Are you a scientist like my dad? Does Dad know you're here? Do you have kids? Tell me everything!" pleaded Freddy.

Ernst kept grinning silently through Freddy's rapid-fire questions and said, "It seems your father hasn't told you much about me."

"We gotta take you home to Dad!" F.M. shouted. "I'm sure he'll be thrilled to see you. Let's go!" And with that, F.M. threw Ernst over his shoulder like a doll.

"Hey, wait, I can get there on my own!" Ernst objected.

"No way!" answered F.M. "You nearly fell down that cliff! Freddy will drive you there in our super-cycle, and I can run behind." F.M. firmly dropped him in the seat and buckled him in. Then Freddy zoomed up the mountain at turbo speed to the Frankenstein family's Palace of the High Winds.

Uncle Ernst looked very nervous. Freddy reassured him, "Relax, Uncle. We're almost there!"

But as they arrived at the palace, they got a distress signal on Freddy's wrist communicator. *Beep beep boop!*

"It's from Riya!" Freddy shouted back to F.M. as he braked.

F.M. leapt up to Freddy and Uncle Ernst. "We've gotta help her!" he said.

Freddy pressed a button on his communicator. "Can you hear me, Riya?"

"Yes, I can hear you, Freddy! Wow, this communicator is pretty cool!"

A proud Freddy smirked and said, "I told you so!" F.M. could almost hear Riya roll her eyes at Freddy.

"I'm here at the base of the mountain near the school. I need your help!"

Darn, thought Freddy. *I want to see Dad and Uncle Ernst reunited. But Riya needs our help!*

Ernst hopped out of the super-cycle. "It sounds like you boys have an important rescue mission! Don't worry, I can show myself in and surprise Victor. I'm so excited to see him after nine long years."

"How sad that they have been apart for so long," F.M. said to Freddy.

"Yeah. That's exactly why I shouldn't attend that school! You'd miss me too much. We should be together every day!" said Freddy.

"Well, you guys go help whoever this Riya is," Ernst shooed them away. "I'm sure I can find my brother in his laboratory! Which way to the lab?" Freddy pointed him in the right direction, and as Ernst started hiking up, F.M. saw a smirk on Ernst's face that seemed a little creepy.

VROOM!

F.M. yelped as the super-cycle lurched forward and back down the mountain.

Chapter 5:
To Rescue a Unicorn

Freddy and F.M. found Riya in her tiger form with a large creature whimpering behind her.

"Is . . . is that a unicorn?" asked a giddy F.M.

Another creature? Freddy thought. *I knew there would be one!* "I told you so! I knew the mountain is attracting fantasticals!"

Riya sighed and reminded him, "Um, it was ME who told you about the mountain's power."

The unicorn moaned sadly as it frantically tried to get free. "Shhhhhh. We're gonna help you," said Riya gently. But every time her claws got near the fence to free the unicorn's hoof, it would cry out with fear.

"I think your claws are making it nervous," said F.M. "Maybe I can try to get it out with my super strength!"

F.M. was excited to help yet another nice monster. But as he gripped the fence, he heard children start to come out of the schoolyard nearby. "Oh no! I'm scared those kids will see me, or maybe even scare

the unicorn more," said F.M. However, he didn't know they'd already been discovered. Not far away, a girl was watching them from high up in a tree. The girl stared with wonder at the sight of a tiger, a unicorn, *and* a giant monster.

Just then, F.M. saw her in the trees, looking at him. "Aaaaack! A human saw me!" he yelled with fear. The shouting only made the situation even worse, causing the unicorn to thrash around.

"The unicorn is moving too much to rescue it," Riya said. "We have to help it calm down!"

"Wait, I've got an idea!" declared Freddy. He dug through his backpack and pulled out a bunch of wires and metal parts.

"What's he doing?" Riya asked F.M.

"Just watch!"

After a frantic minute, Freddy held up a weird-looking machine with a big antenna and lots of dials. "It's a moonlight-powered radio device! This will send radio waves of music to calm the unicorn. We just need a speaker to play the music!"

"Where are we gonna get one of those?" asked F.M., scratching his head.

Freddy grinned and pointed dramatically at F.M. "You're the speaker, big brother!"

Riya and F.M. looked at each other, equally confused. Freddy turned a knob. "I'm sending the signal to the metal plate in your head right now. Just open your mouth!" F.M. could feel a funny buzzing in his head and so he opened his mouth. And music came out! "I turned F.M. into an FM radio!" Freddy said proudly.

F.M. started dancing to the rhythm, somewhat clumsily. Riya laughed and joined in, and the girl in the tree also giggled and swayed to the music. "It's working!" whispered Riya. "The unicorn is starting to calm down."

Freddy grinned. Riya gently approached the unicorn, still distracted by the music, and tore the fence open. Then the unicorn carefully pulled out its hoof. Working together, the three of them had rescued the fantastical!

Chapter 6:
Sleepy Sparkles

The freed unicorn reared up with joy. Freddy turned off his radio device, but F.M. kept dancing until he realized there was no more music. He blushed but was happy to have helped a nice fantastical. He suddenly remembered the girl in the tree and saw that she was smiling too.

Riya looked up at the unicorn and said, "The S.A.S.S. did an amazing thing today!" The unicorn was so happy to be free that sparkles started to swirl out of its horn.

"Uh-oh. Those had better not be *magic* sparkles. Magic messes up everything!" said Freddy.

Riya frowned at Freddy and said, "Well, I'm magic and I was good at fixing things today!" The sparkles swirled faster and in every direction. Freddy really started to worry, but then said, "I feel sleepy. Oh . . . no . . . the magic . . ." His eyelids started to feel heavy, and he lay down.

"Huh, that's strange," Riya said with concern. The unicorn saw how worried Riya was and stopped making sparkles. But it was too late. They had spread far and wide. Even the schoolkids were falling asleep.

F.M. started to feel tired too. Even at his giant size, the magic was affecting him. "Riya, you have to tell Dad. Quick!" He wanted to lie down but first looked up for the girl in the tree. She had fallen asleep and was starting to fall off her branch! "Gotta save . . . the girl . . ." said a sleepy F.M. He used his last bit of energy to lunge forward. He caught her just in time, then fell asleep right after, snoring softly as the girl slept right next to him.

Riya sent a signal for help to Victor. The magic was spreading farther and farther. She climbed up the fence to check on the schoolkids. *Why hasn't the magic worked on me? Maybe because I have magic powers too*, thought Riya. *The sparkles must have put the whole town to sleep! Everyone but me!*

Victor's voice rang out from her wrist communicator. "Riya, are you there? Are you guys okay?" She had to admit Freddy's invention was handier than she had thought. "I'm here! But Freddy and F.M. have fallen asleep from unicorn magic!"

"Unicorn magic? Riya, I can track your location using your wrist communicator. Stay right there and I'll come to you!" Victor grabbed one of his flotation bubbles and a control device. He quickly opened the roof to his lab and hopped in the bubble to float down the mountain. But Victor never saw his brother Ernst waiting right outside the lab to sneak in.

Watching Victor float away, Ernst snuck into the lab and marveled at all the inventions. "Hee-hee!" Ernst giggled. "I didn't even need to trick him out of the lab! Now I can steal all these amazing inventions and make myself a fortune! He'll never even know it was me!"

Ernst started grabbing all the devices he could hold. But all the clanking noises he made alerted Igor, the Frankensteins' pet monkey. The curious monkey ran to Victor's wife, Shan, who was out in the courtyard, and pulled on her sleeve. "What's gotten into you, Igor?" asked Shan.

"Eeep! Eeep!" Igor squeaked and pointed to the lab.

"Something's wrong in the lab? I thought Victor was in there. Let's go investigate!"

Ernst could hear them coming toward him. "Drat! I've gotten too far to be caught now!" Ernst pressed all the buttons he could find on the wall. One button slammed the door shut before Shan and Igor could even see him!

"Victor? We're locked out! It's me. Let me in!" shouted Shan. "Unless . . . that's not Victor in there." Igor shook his head. "Igor, I have a bad feeling about this."

Chapter 7:
Unicorn Licks and Dirty Tricks

Riya watched over her sleeping brothers. The unicorn stayed nearby, looking at her, no longer afraid of her. "You're free, you can go now," said Riya. "Don't worry about me, I'll be okay."

But the unicorn was limping from its injured leg. Riya said, "Hold on, friend. I'm sure Victor will be here any minute. And he will know what to do about your leg, about Freddy and F.M., and about everyone else!" Riya started to cry. "I promised Victor I'd look after them, and now I can't help them!"

Victor's voice rang out. "I'm here!" But Riya couldn't see him. "Look up, Riya!" There he was floating down in one of his orange bubbles. Victor guided it with the controller and down to Riya, and it popped as he landed. Riya ran over and gave him a big hug. Victor hugged her back and dried her tears.

"I'm so sorry I couldn't protect the boys like I promised," Riya said.

Victor smiled warmly. "What do you think you're doing right now? You called me for help and stayed with them. That's the best thing to do in an emergency! I'm so proud of you." Riya smiled and calmed down. "I'm here now, and we will figure this out together. Now tell me everything that happened."

Riya talked as fast as she could. She told the whole story about the unicorn being trapped. About Freddy and F.M. and her working together to free it. And about the magical sparkles that put everyone but her to sleep.

Victor said, "Well, the sparkles seem to be gone, since they haven't put me to sleep. I think this will be over soon." Victor used a scanner to check the brain waves and heartbeats of Freddy, F.M., and the girl from the tree. They started to move.

"They're waking up!" Victor announced. Riya looked over the fence and could see the children stirring too, some of them in funny positions. Or with drool all over their face. Or with leaves in their hair. But they were all just fine and safe.

Just then, the girl on F.M.'s shoulder woke up. *Uh-oh*, thought Riya. *F.M.'s not going to like this.* But the girl was delighted to see F.M. and shook him awake. He was startled to have a human girl in his face.

Victor said, "You're okay, F.M. And apparently you've made a new friend." F.M.'s eyes were still as big as soccer balls to see a human that wasn't Freddy so close.

"Thank you for catching me!" she said and shyly gave F.M. a big hug before running back into town.

F.M. sat in shock for a few moments until he snapped out of it. "Hey, is Freddy okay?"

"Yes," said Riya, pointing at Victor. "Dad says he'll wake up soon." Victor stopped and smiled to himself. This was the first time Riya had called him "Dad."

The unicorn limped over and tried to help by
licking Freddy's face. Freddy awoke to his own drool
on one side of his face and unicorn spit on the other!
He shot up and shouted, "Shoo!" *A fantastical has
messed things up for me AGAIN*, thought Freddy. *And
embarrassed me too!*

"The whole reason for the Supernatural Action
Search Squad was to keep fantasticals from ruining
everything," Freddy complained.

"Aw, the unicorn magic only put us to sleep for a little bit," said F.M. "It was just so happy to be free. And look! We're all fine. I think it's awesome that we've helped another fantastical in trouble. The S.A.S.S. should help fantasticals who find their way to this mountain!"

"I have to agree," said Victor. "That's a good cause, and worth a *lot* of extra-credit points." Freddy was thrilled to hear that. *That means we can go on adventures for homework*, thought Freddy. *Awesome!*

Then Victor added, "But it's late and we should help the unicorn's leg before humans find it. Let's go home, kids. I'm very proud of what you did today."

Riya said, "I can hear parents coming to look for their kids. We'd better work fast!"

They all worked together to brace the unicorn's leg. Freddy ripped off a panel to fashion a sled, and they used the super-cycle to pull it back to the palace. As they arrived, Shan ran out to meet them, with Igor on her shoulder. She shouted, "There's someone locked in the lab, and it sounds like they are wrecking it!"

"Who could it be?" Riya asked.

"Another fantastical, I bet," grumbled Freddy. "Oh wait! My motion sensor gadget would have notified me of something sneaking up the mountain."

F.M. tapped him on the shoulder. "Well, we *did* detect someone else earlier! Remember, Freddy?"

"Oh yeah! But why would Uncle Ernst mess up Dad's lab?" he asked.

"Ernst?" Victor asked in shock. "My *brother*? Oh no! That's who's up to no good!"

F.M. and Freddy were surprised. "Wait, our uncle is a bad guy?" asked F.M.

"I'm sad to say he is," Victor replied. "That's why I don't talk about Ernst. I'm afraid that money is more important to him than family."

Shan put her hand in Victor's and said, "Family isn't always who you are related to, darling. We've made a wonderful family and filled this palace with love and kindness."

"That's so true. I'm so proud of how the three of you kids helped each other today. Not because you were a great Supernatural Action Search Squad, but because you were great brothers and sister to each other. Now let's go save the lab!"

"Hurry!" said Shan. "I'll watch over the unicorn while you stop Ernst!"

Wow. I'm so lucky to have a good-hearted brother, thought Freddy. *And even a pretty cool big sister.*

"Come on, little brother. Let's help Dad stop our evil uncle!" said F.M.

Chapter 8:
Evil Uncle Emergency!

Victor, his kids, and Igor rushed to the locked door. They heard Ernst cackling inside as he grabbed gadgets to steal. "It can only be unlocked by the safety controls inside," said a frustrated Victor. He pounded on the door. "You'll never get out of there with my inventions, Ernst! Open up!"

"I can just float away with the best inventions using your bubbles, dear brother!"

Oh no, thought Freddy. *He could really get away with Dad's stuff that way.*

"I'll get us in there!" vowed F.M. He grabbed the handle to pull the door open. He yanked so hard with his monster muscles that he took the whole door off!

"ACK!" shouted Ernst. He panicked at the sight of Victor, Freddy, an angry F.M., and a tiger jumping in, so he turned Victor's mega-magnetomotor on maximum.

The magnetic rays caused the metal in F.M. to send him flying high up to the machine!

F.M. was stuck dangling from his forehead. Ernst was delighted until the inventions in his arms also flew from his hands up to the magnet.

"Oh no!" shouted Freddy. His high-tech backpack flew up to the machine . . . with Freddy attached!

"Hold on, boys! I'll get you down!" shouted Victor.

Riya and Igor ran to Ernst. He threw a barrel at them. Riya leapt over it, but it exploded with sticky goo when it hit the ground.

GLOOP!

Gooey green stuff covered Igor, and Riya landed right in it.

"Dad, we're stuck to the floor!" cried Riya.

"Eep!" shrieked Igor.

Victor tried to reach the magnetic controls. "That's enough, brother!" shouted Victor.

Ernst sneered, "Oh, I'm not done yet!" He threw anything he could find to keep his brother from reaching the controls. Victor had to dodge flying wires, plastic tubes, even a flotation bubble.

Helpless and frustrated, Freddy pouted. "All of Dad's amazing machines are being ruined!" he said. "That unicorn really messed things up!"

"We were the ones who sent a stranger to the lab," F.M. pointed out. "Then we rushed off without even telling Dad. It's our fault!"

"But if the unicorn hadn't put us to sleep, then . . . hey!" Freddy's eyes opened wide. "I've got an idea!"

Chapter 9:
A Unicorn Returns the Favor

An excited Freddy asked, "Can you get my new radio gadget out of my backpack?" F.M. couldn't see where to reach, since his forehead was still attached to the mega-magnetomotor. But even dangling up high, he was able to feel around for Freddy's backpack and stick his giant hand in. F.M. was extra gentle as he carefully pulled out the weird machine. Freddy turned it on and shouted, "Now, open your mouth!"

Once again, the radio signal sent pretty music right from F.M.'s mouth! Victor and Ernst both paused to look up at the music, and a moment later, the unicorn gallantly galloped in. Even with its injured leg, it was happy to hear the song again. Ernst was so surprised to see a real-life unicorn, he forgot to keep throwing stuff.

The unicorn reared up with joy. Seeing Ernst's troublemaking, the unicorn pointed its horn right at him.

"Aha!" said Victor. "F.M.! Get ready to land—and hold on to your brother!" He jumped at the panel and shut down the magnetic machine.

F.M. grabbed Freddy as they fell, and Freddy shouted, "Everyone get out!" right as they landed. F.M. yanked Riya and Igor out of the goo and carried them out. As Freddy raced out with Victor, he could see sparkles starting to swirl out from the unicorn's horn.

"Quick, F.M. Put the door back on. That should keep the sparkles from getting out and putting us to sleep!" said Freddy.

"What kind of weird science is this? Get away, foul beast!" shouted Ernst.

F.M. slammed the door back in place. Victor laughed and said, "The S.A.S.S. really saved the day again."

"It's a good thing we had a fantastical friend to help," F.M. said.

"With magical power to save all our science stuff!" added Riya.

After a while, Riya said, "It's probably safe to open the door now. I'll go first in case the sparkles are still working their magic." Riya crept in to find Ernst snoring and the unicorn standing guard over him.

"Whew! Most of my tech is safe," said Victor. F.M. helped him put Ernst in a flotation bubble. Just then, the thief started to wake. Victor glared and said, "I'm sending you far away, brother. Now all my kids know what a bad guy you are. And now you know how powerful and clever THEY are. They will never let you steal my inventions!"

Ernst grumbled as he floated through the open roof. The family watched him float far, far away.

"It's sad that your brother is your enemy, Dad," said Freddy. Victor nodded quietly.

Shan put her hands on F.M.'s and Riya's shoulders and said, "That's true, Freddy. But your dad has you and me and Riya and F.M. We are more family to him than Ernst."

"Even little Igor too," Victor said. "Wait! Where *is* Igor?"

"I can hear noises from the kitchen," said Riya. They all walked over to see the unicorn in the kitchen. It was eating the family dinner that Shan had made. Igor was riding on its back, throwing food into his mouth! The monkey squeaked with joy at the mess the unicorn made.

They all laughed and laughed. Then Victor said, "Come on, Squad! We have one last mission tonight. Let's figure out how to treat the unicorn's hurt leg."

Chapter 10:
New Friends

The next morning, Victor took Riya, F.M., and Freddy down the mountain. "We should release the unicorn near the place you found it," explained Victor.

"Because the unicorn will best know how to get home from there, Dad?" Riya asked.

"That's right, Riya."

The unicorn's leg looked much better. It was barely limping now. But F.M. gently guided it, so it wouldn't stumble. As they arrived at the school fence, the unicorn nuzzled F.M. He said, "Awww, this wasn't a monster to be afraid of at all, Freddy."

"Sometimes fear is worse than any monster, F.M.," Victor said.

"And some monsters make for great friends!" said Riya.

"Yeah, I guess you're right," said Freddy. And the unicorn agreed, thanking Freddy by planting another giant lick on his face. "Ewwww!" protested Freddy. Riya and F.M. tried not to giggle.

The unicorn trotted off into the wilderness. As it looked back at them, it reared up with joy and just a few happy sparkles swirled from its horn.

Riya looked longingly at the school. "It would be so fun to go to school with other kids," she said.

Victor agreed, "A school education with other kids your age could be good for both you and Freddy."

"But F.M. would be so lonely without me!" Freddy protested.

"Well, the only reason I can't go is because of ALL the humans!" F.M. said. "But I wouldn't be lonely with Mom, Dad, and Igor at home."

Freddy frowned. *I don't want to spend every day with a bunch of kids I don't know*, thought Freddy. He tried to change the subject. "Hey, Dad, the first mission of the Supernatural Action Search Squad was a big success. Can we PLEASE make it a regular extra-credit project?" pleaded Freddy.

"I'll do it if we rename it the Fantastical Friend Rescuers!" F.M. said. "I want to make it about helping fantasticals in need. After all, the yeti was only hungry. Uday was just bored. And the unicorn was trapped."

"Yeah, they did all need help, just like me," said Riya.

"That is a pretty worthy use of your smarts and abilities." Victor stroked his chin. "Okay, we'll talk about school later."

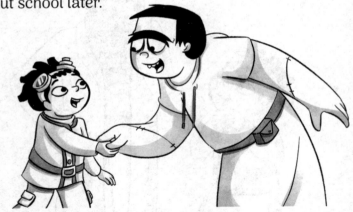

Freddy and F.M. shook hands in agreement. "Our adventures with fantasticals are just getting started!" Freddy shouted.

"That's a great name. Could I join?" Riya asked shyly.

"Well . . . your supernatural powers did come in handy today," Freddy admitted. "Sure, you can join!"

Riya flashed a wide smile, and F.M. jumped up and down, making the ground rumble.

Victor announced, "It's settled. This will be an extra-credit project! Get the Fantastical Friend Rescuers going. But in the spring, we're going to talk again about you going to this school, Freddy." Freddy gulped with dread. "It's clear that I spend too much time in my lab to properly oversee enough schooling for you and Riya. And the amazing inventions you make prove that you don't need to learn any more from me about science stuff." Freddy was so excited by his dad's pride in his science smarts that he didn't even argue again about school.

As they started to head back to the palace, Riya spotted a bright blue package under the tree the girl fell from earlier.

"Look at that!" said Riya. "I think it's for you, F.M. Open it up!"

A nervous F.M. untied the string and opened the wrapping. "It's a drawing of me and the girl and the unicorn as friends! She made  this just for me?" F.M. blushed. High up in another tree, the girl watched them. She was so happy to see F.M.'s giant grin.

"Hey, big brother, you know what?" asked Freddy.

"What?"

"You're right that fantasticals aren't so bad. But some humans make for pretty awesome friends too."

"I suppose they do," said F.M., as he gave Freddy a big monster hug.

VANDAL SCANDAL

Journey to some magical places and outer space, rock out, and find your inner superhero with these other chapter book series from Little Bee Books!

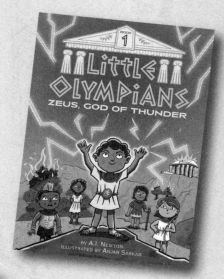

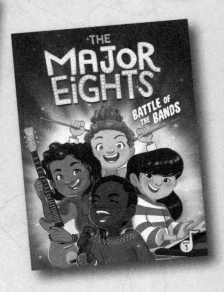

Tales of SASHA
#1
The Big Secret

by Alexa Pearl
illustrated by Paco Sordo

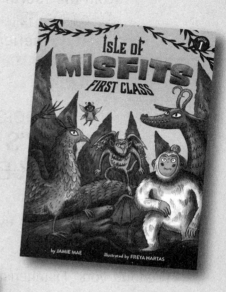

ISLE OF MISFITS
FIRST CLASS
BOOK 1

by JAMIE MAE   illustrated by FREYA HARTAS

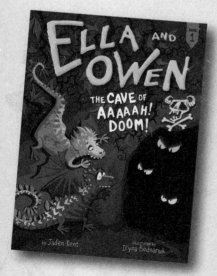

ELLA AND OWEN
BOOK 1
THE CAVE OF AAAAAH! DOOM!

by Jaden Kent   illustrated by Iryna Bodnaruk

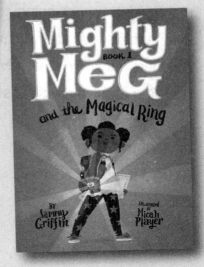

Mighty MEG
BOOK 1
and the Magical Ring

BY Sammy Griffin   illustrated by Micah Player

Read on for a sneak peek
from the fourth book in the
MONSTER AND ME
series.

Chapter 1:
FREDDY'S WORST WEEK EVER!

"**N**o school! I'm never ever ever EVER going to school!" shouted Freddy.

Freddy von Frankenstein had managed to avoid going to school with other kids for years. But on their most recent adventure rescuing a unicorn at the school, his sister, Riya, wouldn't stop talking about how much she wanted to attend classes there and meet other children.

Freddy always had a bunch of excuses ready to tell his parents whenever they brought it up. He complained that the ice on their mountain made it too hard to get there, even though that ice melted in spring. He insisted he learned more from his parents than he could ever learn at school. His latest excuse was that F.M., his big brother and best friend, would miss him while he was there and be lonely with him gone all day.

But F.M. said, "Don't worry, little brother! I'll be with you the whole time!"

Freddy was shocked. "But you always worry about what humans will think of you!"

F.M. gave a big, crooked grin. "You have your wrist communicator, so we can chat all day. It will be just like I'm there!"

Freddy started freaking out, having run out of excuses. But Riya cheered! "Does this mean we can go, Dad?" she asked.

Victor smiled. "I've said many times that you

both need to attend school with kids your own age, and there's no better time than now."

Freddy racked his brain for a new excuse. "Well, with my science smarts, going to a school is a waste of my giant brains!"

His mother, Shan, chuckled and said, "There are plenty of things to learn about besides science, Freddy."

His jaw dropped. "What could possibly be more important than science?!" he gasped.

"That settles it," said Shan. "You'll both start classes on Monday."

❊❊❊

Stomp, stomp, stomp!

The following Friday, Freddy stomped down the stairs early in the morning. Everyone in their home, the Palace of the High Winds, could hear how cranky he was. This was the last day of his first week ever in school, and already he couldn't stand it!

"I'm getting more and more bored every day

I go to that school!" he grumbled to F.M. "I'd be getting smarter if I could stay at home, inventing with Dad . . ."

F.M. followed behind him. As they sat down for breakfast, Freddy continued complaining. "And it's not fair that you have to be so lonely all day."

"Well, I'm not so lonely with Mom, Dad, and Igor to spend the day with. And anyway, you call me all day on your wrist communicator, so I don't even have time to be lonely."

"That's just what I wanted to talk to you boys about," said Victor from across the table. "Freddy, your teacher called to tell me that chatting with your brother all day is distracting you. You're not even paying attention in class! You've given me no choice—hand over your communicator so you can focus on your lessons. You can have it back each day after school."

This horrible, awful morning is getting even worse! thought Freddy.

"Who will I talk to, then?" whined Freddy.

"To the kids in class, silly," Riya answered cheerily. "I'm making all kinds of new friends to talk to at school."

Freddy rolled his eyes. *Who needs to be friends with those boring kids! They don't appreciate my genius, so we've got nothing to talk about*, he thought.

Freddy and Riya packed up their schoolbooks while F.M. handed them their lunch boxes. "I sort of wish I could have a fun day at school," he admitted. "But I'm scared none of the kids would accept me."

Riya patted his back kindly and reassured him, but Freddy was too angry to pay attention. Riya giggled with joy as F.M. waved goodbye to them. Freddy pouted as they made their way down the mountain on his jet-powered super cycle.

Cort Lane is a producer, creative exec, and storyteller with two decades of kids' television experience at Marvel/Disney and Mattel. He has credits on over 50 productions, two Emmy nominations, and two NAACP Image Nominations. He currently serves on GLAAD's Kids and Family Advisory Council, and is working on the new *My Little Pony* series on Netflix.

Ankitha Kini is an animator, comics artist, and illustrator. She loves stories steeped in culture and history. A mix of whimsy, fact, and fantasy brings life to her creature-filled world. When she's not drawing, she likes to travel and to make friends with stray cats. She studied Animation Film Design at NID in Ahmedabad, India, and now lives in Eindhoven, the Netherlands.

ankithakini.com